Blaze and the Gray Spotted Pony

Stories and Pictures by C. W. Anderson

ALADDIN PAPERBACKS

Revised Cover Edition, 2000
First Aladdin Paperbacks edition October 1997

Copyright © 1968 by C.W. Anderson

Aladdin Paperbacks
An imprint of Simon & Schuster Children's Publishing Division
1230 Avenue of the Americas
New York, NY 10020

10 9 8 7 6 5 4

Library of Congress Catalog Card Number: 68-10997
ISBN 0-02-701150-X (hc.)
ISBN 0-689-81741-X (Aladdin pbk.)

to Billy, David and Christopher

Tommy was a little boy who loved horses.
Almost all his dreams were about
horses—all kinds of horses.

Tommy's father and mother and uncles and aunts had never had to ask what he wanted for his birthday or for Christmas. They knew.

Once Tommy got a beautiful horse for his
birthday. It was almost as big as a pony, and
he could ride it. Its mane and coat felt
real. It wasn't alive, of course — but almost.

Billy, who lived down the road, had a beautiful pony named Blaze. Tommy always watched when they rode by. Billy always waved to him and he waved back.

Whenever Tommy got a new little toy horse
he always showed it to Billy. Billy said
they were very nice and looked real.

Sometimes Billy let Tommy ride on Blaze as he led him over the fields. He taught Tommy how to sit in the saddle and hold tight with his legs.

16

Billy also showed Tommy how to take care of a pony. He knew that Tommy wanted to learn this because maybe some day he would have a pony of his own.

Often Tommy ran along beside Blaze when
Billy went for a ride, but after a while
he got tired and turned back. How he
wished he had a real pony of his own!

20

One day when Tommy was out with Billy they
saw a little spotted pony in a field. When
the pony saw them he whinnied and Tommy
whinnied back. He loved that little gray
spotted pony at once.

22

After that Tommy's dreams were only of a
gray spotted pony that always whinnied to
him. Tommy always whinnied back.

One day Tommy's father and mother noticed
that he was very busy building something
in the backyard.

When it was almost finished they came to look
at it. "It looks something like a house,"
said Tommy's father.
"It's a stable for my pony," said Tommy,
"if I get one for my birthday. Gray, with
spots — and alive."

The next day Tommy's father went and asked Billy to help him. "I want to get a pony for Tommy's birthday," he said. "Gentle, like Blaze, but small and gray with spots." He knew it would not be easy.

Tommy's father drove his car and Billy
followed behind on Blaze. They went to
many farms but most of the ponies were too
big for a little boy.

And many were too wild and lively for a boy just beginning to ride.

And none were gray with spots. Both Billy and Tommy's father were sad when they started for home. Tomorrow was Tommy's birthday and they had no pony for him.

Just then Blaze gave a loud snort and started
to pull away. Tommy's father and Billy
turned and saw a trailer going by.
A little pony was putting his head out of
the back. He was gray—and he had spots.

The man driving the trailer saw Billy wave to
him and stopped. While Blaze and the gray pony
made friends Tommy's father talked to the man and
found he was going to sell the pony.

"This pony is too small for my boy now and I must
get him a bigger one," the man said.

So Tommy's father bought the pony. Afterward
he asked Billy to take the pony home with him
so Tommy wouldn't see him until his birthday.

The next morning when Tommy came outdoors
he saw Billy riding toward him on Blaze —
and he was leading a pony! The pony was
gray and he had spots! He whinnied when
he saw Tommy and Tommy whinnied back.

"Blaze found a gray spotted pony for you,"
said Billy.

Tommy soon had his arms around the pony's
neck. "You're mine," he said, "and you're
just like the pony in my dream."

When Tommy rode his pony beside Blaze
through the woods he knew he was the
happiest boy in the world. This was his
very own pony — gray, with spots, and alive.

46